Farmer
Dray's
farm

Apple Tree
Station

Apple Tree
Village

Church

School

This story is about Apple Tree Farm,

Sam,   Poppy,

Farmyard Tales

Surprise
Visitors

Heather Amery

Illustrated by Stephen Cartwright

Adapted by Lara Bryan
Reading consultant: Alison Kelly

Find the duck on every double page.

Mrs. Boot,

some
visitors,

and a
hot-air
balloon.

Mrs. Boot, Poppy
and Sam were having
breakfast.

They heard loud sounds from outside.

Is that the cows?

The cows sounded scared.

They ran out to the field.

Moo!

Moo!

A hot-air balloon had
scared the cows!

"It's landed in our field,"
said Mrs. Boot.

There were two people
in the balloon.

I'm Alice and
this is Tim.

"I'm sorry we
frightened your cows."

"We ran out of gas,"
said Alice.

A truck brought
new gas tanks for
the balloon.

Tim put the gas tanks
in the balloon basket.

Poppy and Sam helped
Tim open up the balloon.

A fan blew air into it.

The balloon grew
bigger and bigger.

"Would you like a ride?"
asked Alice.

"Oh, yes please,"
said Poppy.

Mrs. Boot, Poppy and
Sam climbed in.

Tim lit the gas burner
and the balloon rose up.

The wind blew the
balloon along.

"Look," said Sam,
"I can see our farm."

"We're going down now," said Tim.

20

The balloon took off
again with Alice
and Tim.

"What an adventure!"
said Sam.

PUZZLES

Puzzle 1

Put the five pictures in order.

A.

B.

C.

D.

E.

Puzzle 2

Choose the right sentence for each picture.

A.

"It's landed in our field."
"It's landed on our barn."

B.

The balloon grew bigger.
The balloon got smaller.

C.

We ran out of grass.
We ran out of gas.

D.

The balloon froze.
The balloon rose.

Puzzle 3

Find these things in the picture.
flame   balloon   birds
cow   basket   dog

Puzzle 4

Can you spot the five differences between these two pictures?

Answers to puzzles
Puzzle 1

1B.

2D.

3A.

4E.

5C.

Puzzle 2

A.  "It's landed in our field."

B.  The balloon grew bigger.

C.  "We ran out of gas."

D.  The balloon rose.

Puzzle 3

balloon

birds

flame

cow

dog

basket

Puzzle 4

Designed by Laura Nelson
Digital manipulation by
Nick Wakeford and John Russell

This edition first published in 2017 by Usborne Publishing Ltd.,
Usborne House, 83-85 Saffron Hill, London EC1N 8RT, England.
www.usborne.com Copyright © 2017, 1989 Usborne Publishing Ltd.

USBORNE FIRST READING
Level Two

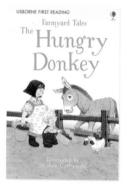

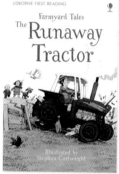

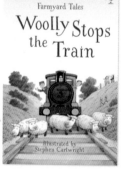

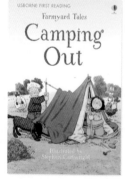